Looking for Livingstone:
An Odyssey of Silence

Looking for Livingstone:
An Odyssey of Silence

MARLENE NOURBESE PHILIP

THE MERCURY PRESS

ACKNOWLEDGEMENTS

For the words and silences of St. John Perse;
for the unerring eye and ear of Paul C. Chamberlain, as well as his unstinting help;
for the comments of Sandy Frances Duncan, my many thanks and great appreciation.

The author gratefully acknowledges the financial assistance
of the Guggenheim Foundation.

§

The publisher gratefully acknowledges the financial assistance
of the Canada Council, the Ontario Arts Council, and the Government of Ontario
through the Ministry of Culture and Communications' Ontario Publishing Centre.

Cover design: Gordon Robertson
Editor: Beverley Daurio

Typeset in Goudy Old Style and Frugal Sans by TASK.
Printed and bound in Canada.
EIGHTH PRINTING, 2003.

Canadian Cataloguing in Publication:

Philip, Marlene Nourbese
Looking for Livingstone

ISBN 0-920544-88-6

I. Title.

PS8577.087L6 1991   C813'.54   C91-094572-1
PR9199.3.N68L6 1991

———————————

Canadian Sales Representation: The Literary Press Group

The Mercury Press is distributed in Canada
by General Distribution Services

The Mercury Press
22 Prince Rupert Avenue
Toronto, Ontario
Canada M6P 2A7

For the ancestors
who have been silent for too long
and whose Silence is.
Always.

THE FIRST AND LAST DAY OF THE MONTH OF NEW MOONS
(OTHERWISE KNOWN AS THE LAST AND FIRST MONTH)
IN THE FIRST YEAR OF OUR WORD

0300 HOURS

My own map was a primitive one, scratched on animal skin. Along the way, some people had given me some of theirs — no less primitive — little pieces of bark with crude pictures of where they thought I would find what I was searching for. I also had some bones and various pieces of wood with directions incised on them. And a mirror. Where was I going? I had forgotten where I had come from — knew I had to go on. "I will open a way to the interior or perish." Livingstone's own words — I took them now as my own — my motto. David Livingstone, Dr. David Livingstone, 1813-73 — Scottish, not English, and one of the first Europeans to cross the Kalahari — with the help of Bushmen; was shown the Zambezi by the indigenous African and "discovered" it; was shown the falls of Mosioatunya — the smoke that thunders — by the indigenous African, "discovered" it and renamed it. Victoria Falls. Then he set out to "discover" the source of the Nile and was himself "discovered" by Stanley — "Dr. Livingstone, I presume?" And History. Stanley and Livingstone — white fathers of the continent. Of silence.

Livingstone now lies buried at Westminster Abbey because he "discovered" and explored Africa, turning what had been "burning solitudes, bleak, and barren, heated by poisonous winds, infested by snakes and only roamed over by a few scattered tribes of untameable barbarians" into "a high country, full of fruit trees, abounding in shade, watered by a perfect network of rivers."*

Perhaps he discovered something else — the same thing I search for —

bruised by tongue
                    under tooth
lips caress
          before
the cruel between of teeth
crush
      grind
the hard kernels
                    of silence
I have retched
 — oh my mothers —
upon its bile
                whole
swallowed
touch   prod   kick
                      shove
push
      I have —
stroked the kin
                  the stranger
within it
taken it to places secret
with within
from the between of thighs
                              expelled
I have
with the force of full
                          driven it
 — a giant birthing —

from the hiding of its
place
    raw with inside
                smell
of body
smell of birth
        sweet
        clean
clings

some days
        its odour
rank
   upon me
I re
   cognize it
   in its belonging
   know it again

THE FOUR HUNDREDTH DAY IN THE SIXTEENTH MONTH
OF THE TEN THOUSANDTH YEAR OF OUR WORD

1500 HOURS

I had been travelling in circles these past hundred years — circle upon circle — ever widening; as I went I questioned, with very little success, everyone I met about what I was searching for. And what was I searching for? I was not at all sure — had only the barest of intimations of what it might be.

I often dreamed I was showing someone my maps, one by one taking them from my bag. Each "map" is blank — faster and faster I keep discarding them, becoming more and more upset. The last one I take out is an old piece of parchment, covered with markings, drawings and words, none of which I understand. Try as I might though, I cannot make sense of this dream.

"As soon as you see it, you will recognize it." This was what the women told me when I arrived in the land of the ECNELIS. What did they mean by this? When could I expect to discover it? The men were silent; the women laughed at my questions — told me it was not a thing to be discovered, so much as recovered. I showed them my maps — asked them to show me the way — they laughed even more. "What colour is it?" I asked, pointing to the outlines of various strange lands — "green like the fields? blue like the sea or rivers? and how will I recognize it?" Suddenly the women stopped laughing and withdrew to their huts; they remained there for a long time.

By my reckoning they were gone for three months — when they came out they told me it had only been half a day. There was no point in my pestering them any further — I now knew that — especially since they were preparing to go to war. I was a mere distraction. They had been going to war regularly, they told me, ever since they could date their first memory, which was a long, long time in the past. Against the SINCEEL.

"God first created silence: whole, indivisible, complete. All creatures — man, woman, beast, insect, bird and fish — lived happily together within this silence, until one day man and woman lay down together and between them created the first word. This displeased God deeply and in anger she shook out her bag of words over the world, sprinkling and showering her creation with them. Her word store rained down upon all creatures, shattering forever the whole that once was silence. God cursed the world with words and forever after it would be a struggle for man and woman to return to the original silence. They were condemned to words while knowing the superior quality of silence."

In a voice that cracked with age, Bellune, the oldest woman of the ECNELIS, told us this as we all sat around the evening fire. Chareem, the youngest girl-child to have seen her blood that year and come into her womanhood, lifted her hand, her palm facing outwards; Bellune fell silent as she began to speak. "There are some who believe the first act of God was to create the word — primary and indispensable." Chareem's voice, still childlike in tone, never faltered once over syllable or word: "Offspring of God, Word, seamed by silence its shadow." The words were much too heavy and ponderous for a child of her years, but she was at home with them, as if her body, her bones had stretched with them as companions, her flesh rounding out around the ideas they contained. "These people — the word-believers — believe in the power of words — to do magic, solve problems, grow crops; words to live by and die, and more than anything else to banish silence." The girl stilled her words. For a brief moment the men, women and children of the ECNELIS waited. It seemed like we sat like that, in the waiting, for days and days before the words came again.

"Their stories tell of how God, feeling bored, came down to earth one day in the shape and form of a man and offered a choice to the first person he saw — a poor peasant: the word of God or silence. Quelled by the splendour of God made man before him, and being devout and very frightened, the poor man chose the word of God — believing that silence was the same as being one of the dumb animals he cared for. God laughed, believed himself vindicated, and rewarded the earth with words and more words. And so their ancestors, so their stories tell, mounted armies of words to colonise the many and various silences of the peoples round about, spreading and infecting with word where before there was silence. God rewarded them with an even greater hunger for words to drown out the silence they still sensed in unguarded moments."

A male voice, deep and resonant, now took up the story: "Every hundred years by our calendar, during the month of Cassiopeia, we go to war with the SINCEEL — those whose beliefs differ from ours, about the primacy of word or silence in the beginning of the world. After the battle, and for the next hundred years, the loser is condemned to follow the beliefs of the winner. Where there was silence, the winner imposes the word; where the word, silence."

I was never able to find out what the ECNELIS believed. Had they, believers-in-silence, been losers, cursed and damned to the sacrilege of the word, all the while craving silence; or were they word-believers, secretly vouchsafing their belief with every word they uttered, as they prepared to win again? Was that why I had got such short shrift with my questions?

Abruptly and early one morning I bid them good-bye and left, taking with me my maps, my few belongings, and some food they had given me. My last image of the ECNELIS is of them sitting around a fire sharpening their tools of war — words — for the battle of cosmogonies.

it bound the foot
sealed the vagina
excised the clitoris
set fire to the bride
the temple dance was
                              no more
in the banish of magic
the witch burned
celluloid nipple
                    gripped
by pincers
whirrs round and round
bitch-white
              nigger-woman
black
      Victoria
Queen or Jemimah
whore-wife
virgin-slut
                 across
the ache   in chasm
stretched the word
                      too   tight
                      too   close
                      too   loose
nestled in the flesh
                        grounded
in the or of either

THE THIRD DAY OF THE FORTIETH MONTH
IN THE ONE HUNDRED THOUSANDTH YEAR OF OUR WORD

2500 HOURS

I had been with the LENSECI three years and three days — by my calendar — before I knew what the women of ECNELIS meant when they said I would recognize what I was looking for when I saw it. Theirs was a community rooted in a land harsh and hostile to all their efforts at cultivation. They were kind to me, but expected I would earn my keep, so every morning before the sun was up, I left with the women for the fields, to return exhausted some twelve hours later. Six to six — my labour stretched the hours into days, the days into weeks and months, the months into years, until it seemed like one hour was the same as one year or one hundred years. Between long, hot, dry spells when nothing grew, and the sun baked the red clay soil to my feet, and periods of torrential rains which washed me clean, my labour had erected an empire of time. They weren't very helpful, the LENSECI, they knew nothing about what I was looking for and cared even less: brute labour had erased all thoughts beyond food, sex and sleep, and my questions dropped like dead weights in the abyss of their ignorance.

Not knowing where next to go, I remained where I was, labouring in the body until I came upon him. A ghostly shape standing tall and thin among the stalks of cane: I rubbed my eyes, looked again — he was still there, pale, gaunt and naked. Dr. Livingstone himself! I recognized him — knew him again. I reached out to touch him, shaped my lips around his name — "Dr. Livingstone" — and as quickly he was gone. I had to follow him — I knew it now — in his footsteps to the interior. I hadn't known it, but this was the sign I had been waiting for.

Maybe the women of the ECNELIS had been wrong after all: they had said it was something to be recovered, not discovered. If I could only discover this as yet unnamed thing, it would be mine, I believed. I could possess it — make it my own. Wasn't that what Livingstone had done? And Prince Henry the Navigator. And Columbus. And Cartier. And all those other explorers. Discover and possess — one and the same thing. And destroy.

It was time to leave — Livingstone beckoned, and I had to move on. So, some hundred years later, I prepared to leave the LENSECI.

Just as I was setting out late one evening, an old woman approached and gave me a bundle of food; it would last me many days, she said, scurrying into her thatched hut to return with a map which she thrust at me: it had been her mother's before her, she whispered from behind her hand covering her mouth, when they had made the same journey together, "and her mother's before her," she continued, still hiding her mouth, "and on back... " I looked at the map; the old woman kept pointing to a particular spot on it. In the fading evening light, I could barely make out the faint brown ink outlining the still unknown land her gnarled finger touched. All along the map's edges someone had drawn monsters and exotic creatures — some with two heads, others with human bodies and monster heads — filling all the blank spaces with these drawings. "What are those?" I asked, pointing to the pictures. She smiled from behind her hand and shook her head. She didn't know any more than I did. Then she reached out and touched my chest — over my heart. She repeated this gesture several times — touching the map, then touching the heart area of my chest. She meant for me to go where she pointed — that much I now knew, but where it was and how to get there, I still didn't know. I nodded, smiled at her, took the map and put it in my knapsack along with all the others I had collected. Before I knew it, she leaned over, put her slack wet lips against mine in a gentle kiss, smiled her toothless smile again, and was gone.

I thought of Livingstone — how he would have loved this challenge. His challenge was merely a continent; mine was — well... it was too soon to say. And what support he had! — African porters to carry his baggage, to interpret and lead the way —

What did I have? Myself. A few tattered maps, some food, and my stubbornness. His supplies alone would have kept me going for centuries — a thermometer; quinine for malaria; a magic lantern to frighten and impress the "savage heathen" with God; guns for killing — a rifle *and* a double-barrelled, smooth bore gun; ammunition; several changes of clothing; a Nautical Almanac; Thomson's Logarithm Tables; and, of course, the "good book" — The Holy Bible — the word of God. Not to mention his tent *and* sheepskin blanket for those cold nights in the Bakota plateau, as well as sugar, coffee, and tea — "elevenses" in the deep, mysterious African jungle! And to keep him on course, a sextant, a chronometer watch — *with* a stop second hand no less! an artificial horizon, *and* a compass. And finally his arrogance — his insurmountable arrogance.

With my maps, my body, and my silence, I followed Livingstone —

Beyond the beckon in
                    beyond
the last sea
the ultima Thule
where space is
the page
        blank
ignorance made monstrous
where meet
Alpha and Omega
in one beginning
                    beyond
the side of other we call
nether
        and nothing
begins
comes the explorer
                — wanderer
                — adventurer
                — expert
certified
        in silence
in ancient schools
their mysteries
        secrets
        sciences
studied
        — their silences —

cartographer
                mapping contour
and structure
                shape
the serene elevation
of silence
to risk the fall in original
with sin
                precipitate
off the flat-earth edge of
knowledge
                into
the very of silence
to find the bang that was
beginning
                big
beyond
                the wait in horizon
                the straight line margin
in circles
                widening
into ever
from the silence of
                        stone
                        dropped

THE TWENTY-FIFTH DAY IN THE TWO THOUSANDTH MONTH
OF THE TWO BILLIONTH YEAR OF OUR WORD

1000 HOURS

Five thousand years – that's how long I had been travelling when I arrived in the land of the SCENILE, tired but still excited about my search for Livingstone. The SCENILE reminded me of the ECNELIS in their civility and gentleness, but like the LENSECI they made me work for my keep. For the first few hundred years I worked in their library of ancient books – transcribing esoteric script from crumbling old books into newly-bound volumes. It was my ignorance that got me the job, they told me: knowledge of the script meant power in their society, and only a few people were ever admitted to such power. Since I couldn't read their script, I was the ideal transcriber.

I would often question them about my own journey, seeking direction from them. Unlike the LENSECI, they said they understood what I was looking for, but they never gave me any satisfactory answers. The years passed; I was happy with the SCENILE, but knew I would have to move on eventually. So, some nine hundred years to the day – almost – after I got there I decided to leave.

They refused to let me go. Not until I answered three skill-testing questions:

1. WHAT IS THE QUALITY OF SILENCE?
2. WHY WAS DR. LIVINGSTONE BURIED AT WESTMINSTER ABBEY?
3. WHEN STANLEY FIRST MET DR. LIVINGSTONE, WHAT WERE HIS FIRST WORDS TO THE DOCTOR?

I failed miserably.

The quality of silence. All I could think of was Portia and the quality of mercy not being strained — "dropping like the gentle rain." Shakespeare had to have written something about silence, hadn't he? Why hadn't he? Maybe he was about silence. But that wasn't getting me anywhere with the SCEN-ILE. The "good book" was of no help either — that was all about the word being in the beginning — nothing there about silence. So I leapt right in — "The quality of silence is... " I watched them watching me expectantly, "Silence," I said. "The quality of silence is silence," I repeated. Oh, how they laughed, the women especially, and clapped their hands. Was I right or wrong? I still didn't know.

Now to Livingstone — why was he buried at Westminster Abbey? "Well, they couldn't leave him in Africa, could they?" I said, growing bolder. They knew I was playing for time. "Livingstone — Westminster...

"Livingstone was buried at Westminster Abbey... because... because he discovered— "

"Yes, yes, come on, come on," they urged me.

"Because he discovered... Silence!" I yelled, getting right into the swing of things. "He discovered silence — my silence — discovered it, owned it, possessed it like it never was possessed before." This made them laugh even harder — the women.

And the last question — what did Stanley say to Livingstone when he met him? Everyone had now fallen silent — waiting for my answer. No one would meet my gaze — not that I could read the answer in their faces in any case. "When Stanley met Livingstone," I challenged them with my words and my loud voice. "When Stanley met Livingstone, he said, 'You're new here, aren't you?'" This answer brought the women running over to me — the men having wandered away — and they embraced me, rubbing my arms and legs. They touched my face and said I was now one of them.

"Wait, wait," I said. They looked at me, rather puzzled. "What if Stanley had said to Livingstone, as he lifted his hat, in the jungle... in the African jungle... after travelling God knows how many miles — what if he had said, 'Dr. Livingstone, I presume?'" More laughter.

"I presume," they repeated.

"I presume," I repeated.

"I presume," we said together.

"We presume, we presume, oh, how we presume! Long live I presume! Long live Dr. Livingstone, Stanley and Silence!"

Now we all began shouting, "I presume! I presume!"

We then feasted, danced and feasted some more; finally they let me go, but not before giving me two anagrams. When I solved them, they told me, I would learn something about what I was looking for.

gulag and bantustan
                              elegant
balanced
              equations of silence
                                        precise
explode
atomic and sub-atomic
                              particle
and wave
              of silence
tongue-tied   rests
in the 'is like' of simile
defies the is
              in silence of
                              star
                              planet
                              galaxy
                              red dwarf
                              red shift
                              black hole
silence is
silence is
silence is
              the rings of Saturn
              the backside of Uranus
words
in the effort of silence
the off limits of imagination
                              reaching

for the more
             in silence
to force pattern on eye
                        texture and
form
     (of silence)
mass and density
                  cubic
silence
       volume and quantity
theorems
         of silence
the measurable properties
in the stretch
               — leagues   miles   fathoms
of silence
          arcane
out
    along its length
across
      the infinite of its breadth

             fingers intuit
                     sift
             air is winnowed of
                           chaff
             words —
                   kernel and grain
             to leave behind
                           silence
                           sacred
                           secret
             profane in word
                           its utteredness

SOMEWHERE IN THE DARK CONTINENT

"Now see here, Stanley – this is *my* expedition – you just can't horn in on it like that, you know. I want all the glory for myself, my God and my Queen. Those falls were worthy of her name, now, weren't they?"

"Dr. Livingstone, I only wanted a piece of the action – there's a whole damn continent out there for the taking. You don't have to be so selfish."

"You call *me* selfish – after all I have done for God, my country, and for the natives – after I risked my life to bring them to the one God, the true God, the only God – materialism! – you call me selfish? Go and discover something you can call your own – give your name to a new race, a river, a mountain – whatever – conquer a piece of history you can call your own, but leave me alone."

"Gimmie, gimmie never gets – come on, let's be men about this, Livingstone. You and I will be forever linked, and Stanley and Livingstone has a better ring about it than Livingstone and Stanley – so there."

"Why are you stopping, men – carry on, carry on!"

FOR EXACTLY TWO HUNDRED YEARS NOW I HAD BEEN HAVING THE SAME TWO RECURRING DREAMS – SOME-TIMES ON ALTERNATE NIGHTS, SOMETIMES ON THE SAME NIGHT –

HE – LIVINGSTONE – AND I COPULATE LIKE TWO BEASTS – HE RIDES ME – HIS WORD SLIPPING IN AND OUT OF THE WET MOIST SPACES OF MY SILENCE – I TAKE HIS WORD – STRONG AND THRUSTING – THAT WILL NOT REST, WILL NOT BE DENIED IN ITS SEARCH TO FILL EVERY CREVICE OF MY SILENCE – I TAKE IT INTO THE SILENCE OF MY MOUTH – AND IN A CLEAR-ING IN A FOREST HE SITS AND WEEPS AS STANLEY COMFORTS HIM –

"I SAY, OLD CHAP, WHAT'S THE MATTER?"

"MY WORD, MY WORD IS IMPOTENT– "

"FUCK THE WORD, LIVINGSTONE."

"THAT'S WHAT I'M TRYING TO TELL YOU, OLD CHAP– "

"I KNOW WHAT YOU'RE TRYING TO TELL ME, LIV-INGSTONE, AND I SAY FUCK THE WORD – A CONTI-NENT AWAITS US – EAGERLY – LIKE A... LIKE A WHORE!"

"AND YOU A JOURNALIST, SIR – HOW CAN YOU SAY SUCH A THING? DON'T YOU SEE, STANLEY, WITHOUT MY WORD, THE CONTINENT IS BEYOND ME – BEYOND US?"

IN MY SECOND DREAM I AM HUGE AND HEAVY, BLOWN UP LIKE A SOW ABOUT TO FARROW – THE FRUIT OF HIS WORD. PREGNANT FOR ONE THOUSAND AND TWO YEARS – MY LABOUR AN AGONY THAT LASTS FOREVER AS I STRUGGLE TO BIRTH – NOW SQUAT-TING, NOW KNEELING, NOW SITTING, NOW WALKING – I GROAN AND GRUNT LIKE THE ANIMAL I AM, KEEN-ING AND WAILING I TRY TO BIRTH THE MONSTROUS PRODUCT OF HIS WORD AND MY SILENCE – CON-CEIVED IN THE SILENCE OF MY OWN, MY VERY OWN WOMB.

*Journal entry written on the back of a camel on the sixth day of the
ninth month in the millionth Year of Our Word.*

Out out of my dreams, Dr. Livingstone — go inhabit your
own dreams — your own silences. I become obsessed —
oppressed — impressed? perhaps, with you — a seeker like you
— I'm off to the interior or perish, but I seem to be following
you — in your footsteps — or is it you who follows me — each
becoming a mirage to the other. I am determined to cure
myself of you, Dr. Livingstone
  — of this obsession
  — with silence
  — with the word — your word — engorging itself on my
many, yet one, silence, sucking it dry — the paps, the dried
dugs of my silence that haunt your turgid phallused word —

Was it the word
	In Mary's womb
Exploding
		Or the Silence
Of holy
In the desert that was
				Elizabeth
Seeded with Silence
				Barren
Shrivelled womb
			Refusing
The swell and
			Split
In seed until
			Silence
Welcomes
The hungry word
			In again
And again
		The womb
Oasis of Silence
			Blooms

Friday the eighteenth day of January, 1859
London, England.

Dear David,

I have written so very many letters to you — I have now lost count... all I have received in return from you is silence. And more silence. I know your discoveries are most important — to you, to the nation, to God and our Queen, but what of me, David? Why is silence my lot? Why? I pray you leave the continent — let it be — free yourself of it; it is damned and will but curse you for your labours.

I, who have travelled the Kalahari with a child at my breast and one in the womb to be with you, want more than silence. I demand more than silence — I am entitled to more than silence. I have made my home, my only home in your country, the country of your God — silence — and how I abhor it.

I am your wife, David, and I am jealous — very jealous. Can one be jealous of a country — a continent? Oh yes — oh very very yes — and I am jealous of Africa — of the massive, impenetrable and continental silence she has now come to symbolize to me. Oh, David... she has you, her silence possesses you as mine never has, and you penetrate her — up her rivers and falls, through her undergrowth, her jungles — to what end? To discover what? My howling silence.

When the Silence of Shupanga claims me for the last time, David, you will weep for me and my silence, my very small silence that now flails at that larger Silence. Oh, how I long to hear from you, David — to break the sentence of my silence... I bid you "a hundred thousand welcomes." And only one good-bye.

I remain

Your dearest and most faithful Wife
in God and Silence,
Mary Livingstone

In the beginning was —
nothing
     could
     would
be
  without Silence
         culture
nurturing the paradise
     the parasite in word
with the upon of
        hang
        wait
        depend
Word and Silence feed
           the share
in need
    wed
content
    with the conspire
in symbiosis —
       embryo word
clasped
     clings to the surround in
Silence
    divided by the Fall
in word into
      silence minus word
wanting Silence
      cleft
       one

into two
              halved into twin
                     into split
                                    severed
by the Lord in word
                          whole
original

In the beginning was
the ravage
              in
word inside time
                     inside
History
        Silence seeks the balance
in revenge
the cut in precise
                          cleaves to the ever in Word
seeking to silence
Silence

SOMEWHERE, AFRICA

"You know, Stanley, I must say the newspapers did do me justice: 'the greatest triumph in geographical research.'* An apt description, wouldn't you say? A gold medal from the Royal Geographical Society, keys to half a dozen cities, an honorary doctorate at Oxford, an audience with our beloved Queen — what more could a man want? Listen to this, old chap — '... this truly apostolic preacher of Christian truth... Seldom have savage nations met with the representative of English Civilization in such a shape. He came not for conquest or for gold, but for love of his fellow men.'* Ah!"

"I say, Livingstone, have you ever thought of how history will judge you?"

"Bugger history — excuse my language. I have discovered a geography all my own — unique — the geography of Silence and the geography of the Word, and that, my dear Stanley, is what I will be remembered for."

"See here, Livingstone, this map is all wrong — to reach the source of the Nile, we should be going that way, not this way. Confound it — these maps are utterly unreliable."

"Yes, yes, you're quite right, Stanley — that's why I always travel with native guides myself — don't know where we would be without them. Between you, me, and the jungle, Stanley, it is they who should get the credit — don't you agree?"

"You're right, Livingstone — you're right, but they wouldn't know what to do with it. What would they do with keys to European cities and honorary degrees? And can you imagine them meeting the good Queen Vic herself? Ha! Come on, boys — we're off again."

word-track
spore of silence
from hole to hole stinking with
                              every
nook-dark
peep-hole   crevasse and
                         cranny
fleeing the crack in certain
                           retreating
into never
from the legend in Land's End
to the timeless in Timbuctoo
the ripe stench of despair
                            clings
seeking the first in source
the source in unravel
the unravel in universe
where suck   pull   and tug
of word-spore
              tease
seduce the traveller
                      weary
with the conviction of word
the gravity of silence
                      black
with collapse
              beckons

sharing the pull in attract
                              Word
and Silence
                    balance in contradiction
Silence and Word
                    harmony of opposites
double planets
                    condemned
to together

THE FIFTIETH DAY OF THE FIFTIETH MONTH
IN THE FIVE BILLIONTH YEAR OF OUR WORD

0100 HOURS

I had been travelling for some two million years when I got to the land of the CESLIENS, some thousand years after I had been with the SCENILE and scored full marks for my answers to their skill-testing questions

The CESLIENS, thank God, weren't into skill-testing questions. In fact, they weren't into anything — they didn't talk. They could, but they refused, and since they refused, I never did find out why there were silent. It was, however, a relief to be silent and not talk. I had grown tired of my own words: they were of no help in my quest for Livingstone.

It was with the CESLIENS I learnt about silence and how wrong, how very wrong, I had been about it. Nothing in nature is silent, they taught me, naturally silent, that is. Everything has its own sound, speech, or language, even if it is only the language of silence (there I go again — "even if"), and if you were willing to learn the sound of what *appeared* to be silence, you understood then that the word was but another sound — of silence.

The CESLIENS weren't silent — not really. In the fifty years I spent with them I had learnt their tongue — the language of their silence; then it no longer mattered why they were "silent." I had become fluent in their silence and by then knew I had to move on again — Livingstone was on my mind — "I will open a way to the interior or perish."

On my last day with them, the CESLIENS held a ceremony for me. When the sun was about half an hour away from disappearing altogether, we — the women and children — gathered underneath the Tree of Tears — the great Samaan tree. (This tree, the CESLIENS told me, always wept at night,

a red rain that kept the earth under its branches sacred.) I had
noticed before, but it struck me again, as if for the first time,
that this was a land of stark extremes — heat or cold — and
intensity of colour knowing no relief. Above me the Tree of
Tears spread its fine-wrought tracery of leaves against the
evening sky — black against indigo — everything sharpened
into contrast and relief in this land; below me the deep red
earth stained an even deeper red by the long, evening shadows.
And between sky and earth, expanding ever outward from its
nucleus — palm skin against drum skin — defining the outer
edges of silence, drum sound.

The oldest woman of the CESLIENS, Mama Ohnce
(pronounced wonce) drew a circle in the earth with a stick.
We were all silent. I was afraid, not knowing what to expect,
and as usual I wanted to ask questions — real questions, with
real words — using my own language. I don't know why, but
it felt safer than their language, the language of silence.

Two women then took me and walked me round the circle
Mama Ohnce had made. Ah, the circumference! I thought,
my little mind scurrying busily all over, trying to figure out
what was going on. Mama Ohnce took a piece of string, put
one end under a rock at one point along the circumference,
stretched it across to the other side of the circle, and held it
in place with another rock. I smiled to myself — I recognized
this as well — the diameter, of course. She then went to the
centre of the circle, cut the string in two and offered me one.
I reached out, held it and screamed, dropping the shiny green
snake that now wriggled across the ground. I broke out in a
cold sweat that stank of my fear; I could still feel the snake's
cold, scaly skin on the palm of my hand which I now wiped
and wiped against my coat. Mama Ohnce reached down and
picked up the snake — it became once again an ordinary piece
of string. Once more she held it out to me; despite my fear
my arm lifted, unbidden, reaching out for the string. When

my fingers closed around it for the second time, I held a wet, slimy birth cord, at the end of which a placenta — a dark rich red — dropped blood on to the already red earth. Sweat covered my body, although the sun had set and it was quite cool; around me the drums kept time and rhythm with the pulsing of my heart. I hadn't dropped the birth cord — merely stood holding it — but when I looked at it again, I saw I now held a piece of string reddened by the earth on which I stood.

Mama Ohnce motioned for me to measure the string around the circle; I did — it went three times and a bit. Hah! I thought, something else I recognized from my previous life — Pi — but I couldn't say anything, of course. Everyone smiled, nodded and walked off. I looked suspiciously at the string lying there on the ground, daring it to turn into a snake again, or a birth cord, or anything.

It just lay there — an ordinary piece of string. What the hell was I supposed to do with it? No one said anything — not even in their language of silence. Pi — three times and a bit — and to find the area of the circle, you multiplied Pi by the radius squared. Pi — three and a bit, 3.1415926 to be exact and inexact, since it keeps going on and on. Randomness or order — which was it? Was that what this was all about — my travels, my search — was it all random, with no order to it? I looked at the CESLIENS standing silent — not really silent, because they never spoke, but silent all the same — watching me.

I picked up the string and made to leave: I hadn't realized it until then, but I was inside the circle, and each time I tried to step out of it, some unknown force hurled me back to the centre. Time and again I tried; time and again I was thrown back to the centre. I then took to running, the better to jump over the boundary of the circle — again and again the force hurled me back, back, back to the centre, until finally I lay there, curled like a fetus, crying, holding the string, snake, or birth cord, or whatever it was — holding it close to me and feeling more and more wretched. I crawled over to the edge of the circle — tried to erase it — if I could only break it, I told myself, I could get out, leave, be free, say good-bye — find Livingstone. Each time I brought my hand to the line — just a line scratched in the dusty red earth of a village in nowhere — a force pushed my hand back, curling it up close to my heart. Now even my hand was betraying me. Knowledge of Pi was of no use to me; none of my earlier knowledge was of any use to me — all I had was the language of the CESLIENS — the language of silence.

Where the thought came from I don't know— it wasn't even a thought — an impulse, perhaps — unbidden — without my willing it — but I began to trace a circle in the earth — around me — with my finger-tip — around and around — scoring the earth deeper and deeper. Now I was safe. Within my own circle — contained by theirs. And inside this circle — my circle — my hand wrote what I hadn't known until then — the solutions to the anagrams the SCENILE had given me: SURRENDER and WITHIN. I didn't understand the significance of the words and had no cause to be pleased with myself. I had done nothing, had willed nothing, but I *was* pleased — so pleased I didn't hear the clapping. The CESLIENS didn't talk, but how they could clap — long, loud applause. I had done something right for a change; I didn't understand it, but they did, and that was all that mattered.

I got up and stepped out of my circle, gingerly walked through the larger circle, and, lifting my feet up and over the boundary, stepped into the arms of Mama Ohnce and the women, who now cried with and for me. I had to be on my way — I could be on my way now — to Livingstone and my Silence — "I will open a way to the interior — or perish." Perish Livingstone!

The traveller seeks
                    contentment
in silence
                    containment
of press of circle upon circle
that cleanses
                    the pollute
                    the profane in word
to confine within small
                              large
— a universe of silence
                         within
body
cell
atom
                         within
word
adding search to reach
wind to spool
               to twist
of thread along the black
stretch of ever
                    into Silence
that mocks the again in know
the word discovers
                    Word
mirrored
          in Silence
trapped

in the beginning was

                          not

word
    but Silence
    and a future rampant
                          with possibility

and Word

THE SIXTH DAY OF THE HUNDREDTH MONTH
IN THE SIX BILLIONTH YEAR OF OUR WORD

5001 HOURS

I had been on the road for some five million years when I got to the land of the CLEENIS; I was tired – very tired – and Livingstone still seemed a long way away. I had seen no one, spoken to no one during the last two thousand years, though I did have communication with things around me – I had learnt my lessons well from the CESLIENS – but I had been lonely, savagely lonely at times, and was happy to see a human face – to meet people.

The CLEENIS welcomed me, and were friendly enough. I had been there barely a hundred years when one of the CLEENIS leaders, Marphan, a magnificent woman some six feet tall with massive breasts and hips, and of a rich dark-brown complexion, came and told me that my time in the sweat-lodge approached.

"My time? In the sweat-lodge?" She smiled and nodded.

"I don't want to go to the sweat-lodge," I said. "I'm tired, and just want to rest – I've been travelling for a long time– "

She smiled again, all six feet two hundred pounds of her, and quietly but firmly said, "All visitors to our society must go – the day after tomorrow your time in the lodge begins. You should spend the time before then thinking of three words you wish to take into the sweat-lodge with you."

"Three words?" I sounded like a fool repeating everything she said – "what do you mean?"

"In the lodge all words leave you... " she paused, "except the ones you choose." She explained all this very patiently, as if I were a child, or a simpleton. "Before you go into the lodge, you must tell me your words – these are the words that will see you through."

"See me through?" There I went again repeating her words. "See me through what?"

She smiled at me once more — "You'll see."

Hell, shit and damnation! This was all I needed. It was bad enough having to learn to "talk" without words — now all my words were going to leave me. And how could words leave you — was I going to forget them? Was that what Marphan had meant? I was utterly confused *and* angry, but didn't have much time to figure it out, since the following day the women came and took me to a hut, where they bathed me in scented water filled with herbs and flowers. When that was done, they rubbed me with fragrant oils, caressing and massaging me all over. I had heard about the sensuality of the CLEENIS women, but before this had not seen much evidence of it. As their hands moved over my body, loosening tired, aching muscles, I knew their reputation to be well-founded. These hands spoke a language to my body — every cell within me released its ancient and collective wisdom. No longer was body separate from mind and spirit — under the hands of the CLEENIS women they were one, and, yielding completely, I surrendered. When they were done they made me drink lots of water, and sent me back to what had been my home for the last hundred years — a small hut set apart from the other dwellings. As I lay thinking of the power of the hands of the CLEENIS women, I wondered whether Livingstone had ever had such an experience.

All night long I lay there, on my grass mat, thinking, as Marphan had instructed me, of three words to choose to remain with me after all others had fled. "Kill" — there was a word that was definite and sure, much surer and predictable than the word "love" — so evanescent and amorphous. There was a finality in "kill" that was reassuring. I quickly discarded it, though. I wanted words I could touch and feel; words to taste and love like the women of CLEENIS had loved me earlier; words that didn't possess me — didn't own me — like my obsession with Livingstone did; words free, untouched, untarnished by any previous activity. Virgin words! Clean like a new-born baby. "Plunge," "thrust," "cut" — hard words — these and others like them were the only ones that came to me that night, their hard edges cutting a swathe through the silence that surrounded and enveloped me.

I spent a year — three hundred and sixty-six days (a leap year by the old calendar) — in the sweat-lodge, sweating words. How they fled — rushing from all orifices and openings, words evacuating, escaping — fleeing me — a diarrhoea, ceaseless and unbidden — their harsh, jagged edges ripping and tearing their way through my soft, secret folds — I hadn't conceived them so how could I birth them? but still they came, a torrent of words rushing and pouring through me. I retched — vomiting words, words, and still more words, a noxious pus ran from my ears and nostrils, and through my pores I sweated words until I was so weak I clung to these very words to shore me up, give me strength — and how they fled, these words, as if hunted, and maybe they were — by Silence. For whatever reason they left, leaving me silent, and wordless. Were these both the same thing — the state of absence? Wordless except for my three words which refused to leave: "Birth." "Death." And "Silence."

I would need all three in the sweat-lodge, I had finally reasoned that night, as I lay in my hut and tasted my fear of the unknown and the sweat-lodge. That was all I had — birth, death, and in between silence — all I could call my own — my birth, my death, and most of all, my silence. My words were not really mine — bought, sold, owned and stolen as they were by others. But silence! — such devalued coinage to some — no one cared about it and it was all mine.

Marphan had been delighted with my choice of words, and told me the women would all be thinking of me and my words while I was in the lodge. Great, I thought, just great — I sweat, they think.

And what a rout it was — the rout of the word — leaving the dank dark of my silence, wet, moist like birth, like sex — the wettest of experiences — and a balance to the dryness of death where all moisture flees, like my words now fled leaving a desert, perhaps to bloom again into moisture. Was my silence the desert awaiting the bloom of words, or was it a desert of words that awaited the bloom of silence? I didn't know, but as moisture fled as in death, so did the words, leaving "birth," leaving "death," leaving "silence" — the precious silence.

In the silence — will no one offer me — in the silence of the sweat-lodge — thirst — a drink — in the silence of the sweat-lodge   I dream   a drink   I must — a respite from these words — I dream constantly — from dream to reality back to dream again   moving — something to buy   trying to — bustling hot   the marketplace   so noisy! loud — understand cannot — from stall to stall — what I know   to talk   struggling tomakemywordsunderstand — understood!   market women black skin   looking   strong — so large! telling eyes staring and staring   at me   laughing   dismiss me — waves of hands   articulate   sucking teeth   backs turning — must get cool! too much clothing   pullingtwitchingmoaning   throat tight dry mouth sweat pouring from me   take off — taking off my clothes! must make myself understood naked!   wandering laughing   laughingatme   men and women in the market — "Come child, come — see how my words sweet." "Here now, take a taste, see how these words tasty — a special price for you — cheap cheap," voices bold   raucous   attacking, "You won't get no trouble with these words," the marketplace

pushing and shoving screaming wordlessly crying running through the marketplace fleeing the silence – my silence!
among the words   piled high stalls – all the words of the
world – so many   too many   words   bartering   fierce   bru-
tal – "Your word for mine" dumbstruck – "Your silence for
my word," people falling   falling into a stupor – severe
terminal   people speaking yet dumb – like me – paying
money – believing something of value   the marketplace of
words!   the marketplace of silence! – a respite – some water
please... "psssst," someone calling under the stalls – a child
such large round eyes   at me!?   staring   braids beaded bright
skin so soft   so black   nothing – she says nothing   Silence
the calabash   she's offering... water – water!   reaching out –
water!   to drink   deep   of my own   Silence   drinking and
drinking – is there no bottom to it?   centuries   drinking
crying   lost words speaking   Inolongerunderstand   crying   my Silence   no longer my own   drinking   crying   tears
so many!   too many!   tears   filling the calabash to over and
flowing   across the ages   fast flowing   river so wide!   so
deep!   carrying me   back   back to the source... the source
my Silence

One calendar year after entering the sweat-lodge, I came
awake, curled in the fetal position on the floor, crying and
crying. I was hundreds, even thousands, of words lighter.
Food, dance and love – these were what awaited me, and all
the baths, caresses, massages I wanted. I was sorely tempted
to stay with the women of CLEENIS – sweat-lodge and all –
but too much of a good thing, I reasoned, was not a good
thing.

So once more I left on the trail of Livingstone and the
interior – my Silence.

That break in passion
                    through
into
     Gethsemane of word
                         grief
               plenitude of —
murderous with the mad
                    in tongue
— the Babel of chatter —
                    into
erupt of Krakatau
          Vesuvius
into
     Hiroshima and
     History
split by the divide
in space and time
Silence
          multiplies
                    isolate
separate
          forty times
forty
the sully in betrayal
between notes
                    composes
the improvise in silence
— a symphony
                    of much
and much and
much and
          more

than absence of
                    tongue
                    language
                    speech
of word
                    is Silence
where inquisition of break
                         and
havoc in word
                    confronts
the heresy within
                    silence
accused —
            the anguish
in beat of tongue
                    tortured
to against
            on word
walled with erect
                    in edifice
                    in structure

The Institute of Silence
                         waits
its handmaidens
                    hungered
on silence
            — the word for —
Word

THE HUNDREDTH DAY OF THE HUNDREDTH MONTH
IN THE SEVEN BILLIONTH YEAR OF OUR WORD

4155 HOURS

NEECLIS — land of needlewomen and weavers. I had
heard about their skill, barring none, with the needle and the
loom, and for four hundred years lived with the anticipation
of resting when I came to their land.

I was not disappointed — soft clothes, warm beds, woven
blankets, linens and sheets. These would have been more than
enough to seduce me into staying, but there was also the food
— fresh fruit, succulent meats cooked in fragrant sauces, breads
fresh from their clay ovens, and all in abundance — I hadn't
tasted anything like it in centuries! The NEECLIS knew well
how to feed and nourish the senses, *all* the senses; they had
made an art of it, and willingly shared everything with me.
With their excellent climate, and good location they could,
unlike the LENSECI, afford to be generous.

More than anything else, I was glad of the talk, camarade-
rie and companionship — a welcome break in the isolation,
the aloneness. Much as I loved it, the loneliness oppressed
sometimes. What more could I ask for? good food to spare,
excellent conversation, friendship, and love with Arwhal, the
best needlewoman and weaver of the NEECLIS.

Two hundred years passed; I had begun to relax and take
my surroundings for granted. There would be no challenge
here — no skill testing questions, no circles or sweat-lodges —
the NEECLIS were far too engaged with their weaving and
needle work. They spent long hours discussing problems of
aesthetics — debating designs and pattern, the weight of wool,
the right colours of threads and yarns. From the smallest head
band or woven bracelet to the largest wall covering, the
NEECLIS brought the same concern and attention, and I too

began to enter these discussions, observing how my eye for colour and shape and movement of lines had sharpened. All around were the fruits of these discussions: the outer walls of their houses with their red, yellow, and green geometric designs; hand-woven rugs and carpets covering the floors, as well as tapestries and embroidered cloths. I had come to take for granted that my every waking hour would be an encounter and engagement with beauty. In the calm, almost pastoral, surroundings of the NEECLIS compound, with its well-kept and colourful gardens, such craft seemed just and right.

I grew comfortable in my love of Arwhal and of the NEECLIS, although every so often I sensed the beginnings of a restlessness. The lush, opulent environment was beginning to stifle me, once again I felt the urge to move on, to look for Livingstone — but the surrounding comfort sapped all my energy to do so.

These were my thoughts as I lay one evening with my head in Arwhal's lap, while she reclined against a pile of cushions.

"I want to tell you a story." Her voice interrupted these inner reflections, bringing me back to the present. I smiled and settled myself more deeply into the cushions. Throughout my sojourn with the NEECLIS, Arwhal's stories had entertained and delighted me.

"There once was a girl who had six brothers." Her voice, low-timbered and musical, immediately banished any thoughts of my leaving her. "They were all younger than she was and she always did her best to protect them. One day these boys were playing in the forest and came upon a bush with beautiful red berries. 'Oh look,' said one of the brothers — 'berries. I'm so thirsty and hungry, let's eat some.' 'No,' said another, 'remember our sister has told us we're not to eat the red berries on the bushes in the forest.' 'But these aren't really red — they're sort of purple — and besides I'm hungry and she doesn't know what she's talking about.' 'She does,' another brother said. 'Remember, she warned us about going into a particular part of the forest and we didn't listen to her and fell into a hunter's trap.' 'Well, I'm going to have some of these berries,' the first brother said, and began eating them." I smiled to myself, wriggling my toes in their embroidered slippers, and thought, now here comes the good part.

"The others saw that nothing happened to him so they too began eating; soon they had eaten so much they all felt too full to move, so they all lay down and went to sleep."Arwhal's voice lulled me – I too felt as if I were going to fall asleep. She stroked my head and continued: "Several hours later, the boys awoke and found they had all been turned into roosters – six white roosters with bright red combs.

"When the girl saw what had become of her brothers she wept for a long time, then she wiped her tears and went to visit an old, wise woman who lived in the forest. She wanted to learn how to help her brothers become human again." I now half-sat, half-lay, with my head in the crook of Arwhal's neck. With one hand she continued to stroke my hair, sometimes burying her fingers in it, sometimes gently turning and twisting the strands, her voice weaving a net that held us close. "The old woman told the girl she had to make six shirts for her brothers from the tiny African violets that grew in the forest. Each shirt, the old woman told her, would take her a year to make, and in the six years it took her to make the shirts, she was to be silent and not to utter a word. Six shirts and silence – that was her power – if she wanted to return her brothers to human form."

I sat up suddenly – Arwhal was telling me something important, but I wasn't sure I understood what it was. "She wasn't to say a word *and* she had to weave six shirts from flowers," I said. "That seems a hell of a price to pay for having six stupid brothers who wouldn't listen to her. If I were she, I would kill and roast the roosters over six years —" Arwhal looked at me and smiled; she knew I didn't mean what I said. I was suddenly afraid and anxious. Gently she placed a finger against my lips.

"Would you — kill them? Remember," she continued, "silence does not necessarily mean an absence of sound." I nodded as if I understood. I didn't.

"Come with me," she said, rising from where we lay. There was no preparation for it — "I want to show you something." There never is with betrayal — I followed her — especially when it comes in the shape and form of a friend. Just a walk — down a long corridor believing I was going to see a tapestry she was working on. The next thing I knew, we were in a huge room, ablaze with coloured fabric and yarn, and she was telling me I would have to stay there until I could "piece together the words of (my) silence."

"Bitch! Bitch! Bitch!" How long I yelled and screamed I don't know, and what I yelled I don't care to remember — but I traced her ancestors back to a mule and a jackass and threatened to kill her *and* hang her out to dry. Silence. That was the only response I got; it swirled around me and I remembered she had said that silence did not necessarily mean an absence of sound. I could picture her — straight, proud back, beautifully black face as profound as a midnight sky — walking away with the keys jangling at her waist — a smile on her pointed, pixie face.

How I loved her — the beautiful Arwhal — the bitch! And she had left me. I was alone; I looked around, saw the carpets on the floor, the tapestries on the wall — among all this beauty I was alone. Then I cried — because I was tired and frightened and alone and didn't want to be tested any more... and because... I couldn't bear to admit it, but had to — despite the betrayal, I still loved Arwhal, and she had left me. All alone. I sat and rocked, first howling then crooning my pain to myself, and I saw myself drinking from the calabash of tears the little girl had offered me in my dream in the sweat-lodge. I talked and babbled to myself in a delerium of pain and loss. "Livingstone!" I screamed, "if you have anything to compare with this... this... " I had to whisper the word, "betrayal — this perfidy — I will — " What would I do? "I'll pay you everything I have — *everything*! No — I'll even love you, Livingstone — I promise. Livingstone!" I screamed again, "do you hear me?" Silence.

"Piece together the words of your silence," she had said to me. "Or weave a tapestry." I had argued hard with her when she said this.

"But silence has no words," I countered, my heart racing at the certain knowledge that she was going to leave me. "So, there's nothing to do."

"Then do nothing," she replied, "but if you are wise, you will try and make a quilt — a spread perhaps, or weave a magic carpet that will... well, that is up to you. Weave us something," she had challenged, "as a thank-you for your stay here; weave yourself something — something new — never seen before — using what you have, what is yours," and she bent and kissed me on the lips. The fucking Judas! "Using what we all have," she had continued, "word *and* silence — neither word alone, nor silence alone, but word and silence — weave, patch, sew together and remember it is *your* silence — all yours, untouched and uncorrupted. The word does not belong to you — it was owned and whored by others long, long before you set out on your travels — whore words." Then she had laughed. "But to use your silence, you have to use the word."

"Whore words?" I asked.

"Yes, and there's the rub, my dear," she said, and gently

drew me close and held me — "there's the rub — you need the word — whore words — to weave your silence."

There *was* the god-damned rub, and here *I* was robbed of my freedom once again. Oh, Arwhal, you could at least have warned me... memories of our time together — long walks across stubble-yellow fields; the quiet talk of long cool evenings before the fire; swimming, bathing — playing like children in sun-drenched pools and shaded water holes; reading to each other as we lay naked at the water's edge... watching the noon-day sun play hide-and-go-seek with water-damp bodies — first a flank then a nipple, challenging finger or tongue to follow — now a buttock, next the soft surround of navel, soon the long, swift curve of back... tufted, secret triangles of crinkly pleasure... braiding each other's hair, elaborately trying to outdo the other, how we laughed and talked our way into each other's silence... watching her weave her colours... the dying blaze of the autumn sun gilding the loom, setting fire to the deep reds and browns — the purple of her yarn, and gold-leaf-ing the hem of her heavy, woven dress, her ringed fingers glinting in and out of the loom, her face half gold, half black — liquid — in the shifting evening light. We had shared time and space and bodies — our Silences — with each other — and how I loved her... and how little these memories did to dispel my anger.

I was getting fed right up to the teeth with all this imprisonment and challenge — she could have warned me — she could have *if* she wanted to. I had by now completely lost the trail of Livingstone, and to date the NEECLIS had been of no help in setting me back on course, except for letting me rest — until this most recent betrayal. I desperately wanted to find him — Livingstone — but I had to get out of here, and *there* was the rub.

I lost all sense of calendar time and could only track the

moon through the windows at night. Between the moon and my blood, I figured it had to have been at least seven hundred years I remained in that room with my pieces of cloth, a loom and brightly coloured heaps of knotted yarn. As I worked at unravelling the yarn, or sorting the pieces of fabric, I remembered the story of the young girl weaving the six shirts from African violets for her brothers. I felt angry on her behalf — why did she have to do all the work for her brothers — they deserved to stay as roosters if they were so stupid. I was also angry at the NEECLIS and at Arwhal. (In all the time I was there, she never came once to see me.) I remained angry until I began to understand what she was trying to teach me — that there *were* two separate strands or threads — word *and* silence — each as important as the other. To weave anything I first had to make the separation, and before I could do that, I needed to find my own Silence.

I clung to my anger for a long time — it was very hard to let go of it — but when I began to give it up to the Silence around me, my fingers, as if of their own accord, began to weave. Like the girl in the story Arwhal had told me, in finding my own Silence I was finding my own power — of transformation. As I wove I talked and laughed and sang; I cursed *and* I swore. All to myself. And then I wove some more and came to understand how Silence could speak and be silent — how Silence could be filled with noise and also be still. And finally I understood what Arwhal meant — that Silence does not always mean the absence of sound, because in all that sound — of my own voice — I was able to find and hear my own Silence. And I was ashamed — of how much I had resisted the wisdoms Arwhal had offered me in presenting me with a chance to find my own Silence.

Earlier on in my travels, I had wondered and enquired of the ECNELIS what colour my silence was. Back then I hadn't

known what I was looking for, and now here it was before me
— any colour I wished — a riot — a carnival of colour — I had
my choice. And how I loved the silence of purple — those
purple silences — almost as much as I loved the absolute in
the silence of black, or the distilled silence of white; the burnt
sienna of silence — red, green, blue — colour greeting shape —
pentagram, hexagon, octagon, circle — squares of silence —
and as I worked, my anger left.

When they finally came to get me — when SHE finally
arrived, I had woven a tapestry, and had pieced together a
multicoloured quilt — of Silence — my many silences — held
together by the most invisible of stitches — the invisible but
necessary word. "Look," I said to Arwhal, "a quilt in all the
colours of my Silence — to keep me warm on my travels." We
looked at each other and smiled. We both knew I was now
ready to move on.

I had forgiven her her "betrayal" although the pain of her
abandonment had left its mark. We continued to love each
other, sleeping together under the quilt of my Silence for
another fifty years, until, thoroughly spoilt, I left her and the
NEECLIS. They offered me pillows, sheets, cutlery and even
recipes to help make my journey more comfortable. I was
tempted, but refused them all. They would only burden me
and I needed to travel light. And so early one morning, as the
sun came over the horizon, streaking the sky with red, and
gilding the walls of the compound and houses, I held Arwhal
in one long, last embrace. The sun had turned the tears in
her eyes to little gold globules against her black skin. I turned
swiftly walking towards the east and the rising sun, carrying
only my quilt of Silence and a long wooden staff Arwhal had
made for me. In pursuit once again of Livingstone. And my
Silence.

              Single
              Solitary
              Unitary
Is it?
        this absence —
                        of speech
Or legion
            wedged
In the between of words
A presence
              absent the touch
                        the tarnish
In power
In conquest
              Silence
                        Trappist
Celibate
          seeking
The absolute
              in Virgin
Whole

THE MUSEUM OF SILENCE

Seven billion years – that's how long I had been travelling. I had seen many, many strange things; been witness to even stranger events, but the strangest of all was the Museum of Silence, erected to house the many and varied silences of different peoples. The SCENILE, the LENSECI, the ECNELIS, the NISCLEE, the CLEENIS, even the NEECLIS, and many, many others – their silences were all there. As I wandered throughout this museum, I recognized many of the displays – these silences were mine as much as they had belonged to the people they had been taken from.

"Return them," I demanded of the proprietors. "You must return these silences to their owners. Without their silence, these people are less than whole." They smiled and said nothing. It had been theft originally, I continued, now it was nothing but "intimidation! – plain and simple – extortion to continue to hold the entire store of our silence ransom, demand we pay for it, and give assurances we would care for it," as they had.

It was mine – ours – I challenged, to do with as we pleased – to destroy if we so wanted. They told me the silences were best kept there where they could be labelled, annotated, dated, catalogued – "in such and such a year, this piece of silence was taken from the _____." You could fill in any name you wanted – when and how – it was all the same. It was all there in carefully regulated, climate-controlled rooms.

It was one of the world's wonders, they told me, this Museum of Silence – never had so much silence been gathered together under one roof, and they were proud of it. My silence – our silence – carefully guarded and cherished by them! My silence was now a structure, an edifice I could walk around, touch, feel, lick even – and I did – it was cold, cold to the tongue. I could if I wanted, even pee on it, though that would be difficult, contained as it was behind plexiglass.

"Remove a thing — a person — from its source," I said, "from where it belongs naturally, and it will lose meaning — our silence has lost all meaning." These were my final arguments to the curators. "At the very least," I continued, "we should own our silence." It was ours after all, I told them, and upon it *their* speech, *their* language, *and their* talk was built — solid as the punning Petros upon which the early church, harbinger of silence, had been erected. Ours to do with as we pleased, I repeated, to nourish, care for, or neglect; to let rot, or wither away to dust, chewed upon by vermin. "Ours! Ours! Ours!" I screamed, "to do with as we choose," I dropped my voice, "to break, banish, destroy — to negotiate with — " They laughed — how they laughed, and said nothing, which was *not* the same as silence. They said nothing and laughed.

I spat on the ground and left, but not before cursing them to an eternity of "Words! Words! Words! — empty words, lacking that most precious of qualities — Silence." I would remember — never forget how they had gorged themselves, grew fat over the centuries on our silence. At the front of the building, I sprinkled some white powder — the powder of unforgetting Mama Ohnce had given me. With what remained I drew eight designs on the earth. I would be hearing about them again — I knew it — and I knew what I would be hearing.

As I walked away I remembered the CESLIENS — they had kept and cherished their Silence — given up the word and kept their Silence. They were the richer for it. None of their silence was on display in the Museum of Silence.

How parse the punish
                    in Silence
                      — Noun
                      — Verb
absent a Grammar
how surrender to within
that without
              remains

Silence
          demands the break
the die
          in release
in life

THE FIRST AND LAST DAY OF THE MONTH OF NEW MOONS (OTHERWISE KNOWN AS THE FIRST AND LAST MONTH) IN THE EIGHTEEN BILLIONTH YEAR OF OUR WORD, WHICH IS THE SAME AS THE END OF TIME, WHICH IS THE SAME AS THE FIFTEENTH DAY OF JUNE, NINETEEN HUNDRED AND EIGHTY SEVEN IN THE YEAR OF OUR LORD

SOMEWHERE, AFRICA
0000 HOURS

1st - 15th June — have lost tracks yet again, but believe him to be in the area — I must — will find him soon — somewhere — What is it going to be like, meeting him? Have been trying to imagine it — have even been practising my opening words: "Hello there, Mr. Livingstone"; "Good day to you, Sir"; "Well, fancy meeting you here"; "Good to see you, you old bugger," — they all sounded forced. Would I be cool enough to give him a first rate black hand shake and say, "Yo there, Livi baby, my man, my main man!'"?

20th - 30th June
0600 HOURS

Have picked up his tracks again — he is close — so close I can smell him! — checked my Polaroid camera again. (I had been lucky to get it cheap from a group I met a hundred and fifty years earlier.) I want to record for posterity my first sighting of him.

31st day of June
2800 HOURS

Finally (silence) Dr. Livingstone, I presume? (silence) we meet (silence) he and I (silence) in a clearing (silence) in a forest (silence) somewhere (silence) in time (silence) it doesn't matter (silence) This man of God (silence) and medicine — an unbeatable combination (silence) "foe of darkness" (silence) Shaman (silence) Witch-doctor (silence) Holy Man (silence) Prophet (silence) Charlatan (silence) He (silence) and I (silence) and my silence (silence) — his discovery (silence)

I had been searching for him for an eternity, it seemed — eighteen billion years — the age of the universe; advancing deeper and deeper into Silence, my silence, picking up the odd rumour about him here and there, following tracks — some of them old and stale long before I got to them; I had been locked up, tested, challenged — even betrayed — in my search for Livingstone. He would open "a path to the interior or perish." I followed him, opening a path to my interior, or I would, as surely as he did, perish.

And now here he was — here we were — nothing that had happened to me along the way prepared me for this — he and I... and Silence... my silence. We looked at each other... across a distance of some three feet — the infinite in time — my silence. I looked at my cheap, digital watch — I had picked it up somewhere along the way — it was 2800 hours exactly. I looked at him standing there with his guides, Susi, Chuma and Gardener.

"You're new here, aren't you?" I said, and didn't raise my hat — I didn't have one to raise, and even if I did I wouldn't have — raised it. Which of us reached out first, I don't know — it didn't matter — I took his hand and he mine. This old white man — tall, gaunt — my nemesis — half-blind, bronzed by the African sun, the indiscriminate African sun — malarial, sick or crazy — it was all the same.

(silence) Dr. Livingstone, I presume? (silence) I presume (silence) Dr. Livingstone (silence) I presume — he and I... Livingstone, the discoverer, riding on the adventure in the word that hacks and cuts and thrusts its way through the wet and moist climate of Silence, plunging ever deeper into the heart of a continent... and Silence – the discovered silence – my silence. Or was it the other way around? I, the discoverer – he, the discovered. I had nothing to say to him; after eighteen billion years of travel, what was there to say – what could I say? That I had found what I had started out with? Silence?

How cocky he was – Livingstone – and proud of his discoveries. His face brightened and his eyes shone with excitement as he boasted about his exploits: "You must have heard of my journeys across Africa," he said, "bringing Christianity and civilization to the natives. The Queen honoured me for that, you know, and for my work against the slave trade – a terrible thing, that, terrible!" I let him go on and said nothing for a while. Then I spoke, "You're nothing but a cheat and a liar, Livingstone-I-presume. Without the African, you couldn't have done anything – nothing – and what I did, I did all by myself – no guides, no artificial horizons, no compasses – nothing – not even the 'good book' – just me, me and more me. *That* is true discovery, Living-stone-I-presume. No one, but no one had been there before me to visit – to discover my Silence. And furthermore, while you thought you were discovering Africa, it was Africa that was discovering you." At these words, he bit hard on his bottom lip (I thought he would draw blood) but said nothing. I could tell he was very upset. "By the way," I continued, "did you know those bloody South Africans bombed your town, the one named after you – Livingstone, foe of darkness – let's see, it was in nineteen hundred and eighty seven, I believe, in April to be exact – by the old calendar."

"Did they bomb it because it was named after me?" I had caught his interest again. "They never did like me preaching against their enslavement of the African – those Boers – " he shook his head for emphasis – "a nasty lot they were back then – very nasty lot."

"They still are, Livingstone-I-presume, they still are a nasty lot, but why do you always think you are the reason for everything — you really aren't that important. No, they didn't bomb it because of you, but let's put it this way — they would still be mad at you today." He sulked for a long time after this — just like a little boy — while his helpers made us coffee and a meal. He did know how to travel in style, that Livingstone.

Over coffee I gave him credit for discovering my silence, and bringing it out for all the world to see and cherish and love; I told him how indispensable he had been to this, that were it not for him, I would never have set out on my travels to find my interior — the source of my silence — which was he perhaps. This cheered him up, and he grew visibly happier; he puffed himself up — if he didn't have Africa, at least he had my silence.

After the meal we sat down outside his tent to an excellent cognac — Christian man though he was; and while his helpers stoked up the fire, we began talking — exchanging stories, maps and curios — each trying to best the other for the most outrageous, most outlandish tale. I told him all about the ECNELIS, the CLEENIS and the NEECLIS and many of the other peoples I had "visited" on my travels. The Museum of Silence really had him beat, though — he had nothing, absolutely nothing, to compare with that. We laughed a lot, he and I, and I got Susi, one of his helpers, to take a picture of us both — Livingstone-I-presume and I, side by side on my quilt of Silence, smiling at the camera. We both said nothing for a while.

"I want to tell you about a dream I had, Livingstone-I-presume, while on my travels. Being a man of God you might find it interesting."

"Hmm," was all he said. He seemed sunk in his own thoughts.

"In the dream I stood on top of a very high hill, Living-stone, just outside a city. It was just before the end of the day, and the skyscrapers glistened and shone in that last blaze of light you get with sunsets."

"What's a skyscraper?" I looked at him — of course, he wouldn't know what I was talking about.

"A very very tall building, Livingstone-I-presume, which scrapes the sky — literally. Anyway, it was a wonderful sunset, the sky all smudged and streaked with red and orange, the best ever sunset I've seen. You must have seen some glorious ones on this continent, haven't you?" He nodded. "Suddenly I heard a voice behind me telling me that everything before me was mine. I turned to see who had spoken: a tall white man in a pith helmet and freshly pressed white ducks stood there smiling at me. Now that I think about it, Livingstone-I-presume, he looked a lot like you. Anyway, in the dream I asked him what he meant, and waving his arms at the scene spread out below us, he told me again that it was mine — all mine." Livingstone was listening attentively; before going on I reached for the coffee pot and refilled my tin mug. "So, I asked 'pith helmet' what the catch was — I was suspicious as hell and my voice and attitude showed this. The old bugger just stood there looking at me slyly, pretending not to know what I meant. I asked him why he wanted to give me 'all this' and waved my arms just as he had done at the scene below us. He still didn't answer me, but took off his helmet and mopped his balding head with a white handkerchief. Finally I got really impatient with him, told him to go to hell, and said I was leaving.

"What do you think he wanted, Livingstone-I-presume?"

"Hmm, what's that?"

"You haven't been listening, have you?"

"Oh, yes, it was reminding me of the temptation of Christ in the desert."

"I thought you would say that – but I didn't tell him to 'Get thee behind me, Satan.' I wanted him right up front where I could keep my eyes on him. But you still haven't told me what you think the man in my dream – 'pith helmet' – wanted."

"I don't know – was he offering to make you queen of the city?"

I laughed – "Nothing so simple as that, Livingstone. He wanted my – " I leant over and whispered in his ear. He looked puzzled.

"Silence?" he said. I nodded. "Why did he want that?"

"He was offering me words, Livingstone – if I had words, he said, I could be a witness to all that had gone wrong. I could speak out, condemn – I could even blame them. I couldn't do that with silence, he told me. I was just silent with silence. At that point in my dream, I came awake, and I remember thinking that if he wanted my silence so much, there had to be some value in it – don't you think so, Livingstone-I-presume?" I didn't wait for an answer, and continued. "It is the only thing I have that is not contaminated. My Silence – my very own Silence." Livingstone said nothing. "Well, what do you think?" I asked.

"I don't know what to make of it, although I do agree with what he said to you."

"You would."

"But you're so much more powerful with words, aren't you – "

"Are you, Livingstone? And whose words are you – am I – powerful with?" He and I stared at each other, then he looked away, still not saying anything. "By the way, was it you in that dream, or the devil offering me the keys to the city?" He merely shook his head – which of the questions was he saying no to? – I still don't know.

"You know, Livingstone-I-presume, I'm tired – really tired

of these travels. I have found what I came for — have you?"

"Have I what? and why do you keep calling me Living-stone-I-presume?"

"Found what you came for — and I don't know why I call you Livingstone-I-presume — you look like Livingstone-I-pre-sume, I suppose."

"Hmm... well, I found fame — a name — made history, helped establish civilization — they called me the 'foe of darkness,' you know."

"And what a foe you were." He understood my tone, and gave me a funny look. "Little did you know how close the darkness was, eh, Livingstone-I-presume? I myself prefer 'thin edge of the wedge' as a title to describe you."

"What do you mean by the darkness being close?"

"It would take too long to explain, Livingstone, but let's say the darkness wasn't all out there — in the 'dark continent.' You and your kind carried their own dark continents within them." I was getting to him — I noticed he hadn't said anything about discovering any lakes or rivers. "And what about Victoria Falls," I needled him, "didn't you *discover* that?"

He smiled modestly, "Well, I suppose you could say that — although the Africans did know of it — but I was the first — the first European to—"

"You lie, Livingstone-I-presume. The Portuguese were there before you—"

"Half-castes — not Europeans!"

"Bull-shit! — you made that up so you could capture the glory yourself, and long before you, or any Portuguese for that matter, crossed Africa coast to coast — from Loanda to Quilimane — long before that, Africans had done it — so put that in your metaphorical pipe and smoke it." He shut up after that. For a while.

"Well, what did you discover?" he asked finally. "And by the way, what did you say your name was?"

I laughed. "I didn't, Livingstone-I-presume. Just call me The Traveller — that'll do for now." I looked at him, took a sip of my cognac — "As to your first question — thought you'd never ask. You really want to know?"

"Well, I thought since we were sharing confidences— "

"Confidences shit — I'm sharing nothing with you, but I will *tell* you — Silence— "

"Silence?"

"Silence."

"You discovered silence."

"I did — you want to quarrel with that?"

"No, but— "

"But you're curious — you want to know whether I have written any books about my discoveries, or my exploits — whether I've won any awards, was given the keys to any cities — European, of course — made any money, received any honorary degrees — right, Livingstone-I-presume?"

"Well, that would be proof— "

"Proof of what — you ask for proof that I discovered my Silence — my very own Silence — when you're sitting right there in front of me? You want facts, dates and years — the time down to the last millisecond — don't you? and titles of books like TRAVELS WITH MY SILENCE; or MY LIFE WITH THE CLEENIS, or HOW I BROUGHT THE WORD TO THE CESLIENS — what about MY MEETING WITH LIVINGSTONE-I-PRESUME?"

"That would help."

"Do you know what a fact is, Livingstone-I-presume?"

"Yes — of course."

"No you don't — a fact is whatever anyone, having the power to enforce it, says is a fact. Power — that is the distinguishing mark of a fact. Fact — Livingstone discovered Victoria Falls."

"*That* is a fact."

"*That*, Livingstone-I-presume, is a lie, *and* a fact, because you and your supporters, your nation of liars, had the power to change a lie into a fact. Those falls had a name long before you got to them — you remember what it was — the name?"

"No."

"Of course you wouldn't — I'll tell you — Mo-si-o-a-tun-ya — Mosioatunya or The Smoke That Thunders — remember now? And who first named the falls? The Africans, yet the 'fact' we have lived with, is that you, Livingstone-I-presume, 'discovered' Victoria Falls. Now if *I* had the power, I could make 'Livingstone is a liar and a cheat' into a fact — I could say Sekeletu, chief of the Makololo, discovered the Falls, and *that* would be a fact, Livingstone-I-presume. *If* I had the power."

"All right, all right, I see your point," he said sullenly.

"Livingstone, since we're dealing with facts, I want to ask you two questions. Promise me you'll answer honestly?"

"I am a man of my word." His tone rebuked me and he pulled himself up even taller.

"And how, Livingstone — and how. Now — how many converts did you actually make in your entire time in Africa?" For several minutes there was nothing but silence. Eventually his answer came —

"One, I believe." He seemed to shrink into his tall, gaunt frame.

"Sechele, Chief of the Bakwains?" I added. He nodded. "And he afterwards reverted to his African religion, didn't he?" He nodded again and said nothing. "Second question." He looked at me, his face tight with a mixture of anger and shame. He seemed fearful of what the next question would be, and for one brief moment I let myself feel sorry for him, but it was a cheap emotion — he didn't need pity. "Remember your promise now." I cautioned him. "Didn't you advocate the destruction of African society and religious customs so you could bring European commerce more easily to the Africans, and then Christianity?" The silence between us stretched on for an eternity.

"I am waiting, Livingstone-I-presume," I said finally. .

"Yes, I did, but I had to, don't you see, I had to — my work —" I raised my hand and he fell silent. "You're not on trial before me, Livingstone — but how I wish you were."

"But I had a lot of respect and admiration for Africans —"

"I'm sure you did, Livingstone," I said, pouring myself another drink.

"Read my journals, you'll see what I thought of them, I even — " He fell silent once again before my gaze. I smiled at him and he dropped his eyes. We sat like that for a while, every now and again one of us stoking the fire, until he broke the silence.

"You said you discovered silence — I don't understand how you can do that — discover silence, I mean. It's not a thing like a river, or a waterfall, or a country."

"Oh, Livingstone-I-presume, how very, very stupid you are." He looked all crestfallen again — "Come on, come on, cheer up — have another cognac." I held out the bottle. "It's damn good, isn't it — and don't take it to heart — you're one stubborn son of a bitch and I respect you for it." His face brightened. "You know what they say about you?" He shook his head. "That where there was a blank before you filled in — charted and mapped— "

"And so I did, so I did! — " his eagerness to claim his discoveries was both child-like and overwhelming.

"No, Livingstone-I-presume, you did not. Shall I tell you what you did?" He was all huffy again at my interruption and merely shrugged. "You captured and seized the Silence you found — possessed it like the true discoverer you were —

dissected and analysed it; labelled it — you took their Silence — the Silence of the African — and replaced it with your own — the silence of your word."

"No, no — I insist— " I had not seen him so adamant before — "I broke the silence that was there before and *that* was a good thing — silence is never a good thing..."

"Isn't it now, Livingstone-I-presume? Isn't it? Is that the gospel according to Livingstone?" He made a rude sound under his breath, and shifted his body restlessly.

"You say Silence is not a thing like a waterfall, or a river that can be discovered, but I assure you I have mapped and measured my own Silence to the last millimetre, and it exists, Livingstone-I-presume, let me tell you, it exists — so tangible I can even touch it at times — like this— " I reached out and lay my hand on his. He looked down — my black hand resting on his — scrawny, knobbly and white. We looked at each other.

"I have two riddles for you, Livingstone-I-presume — a riddle, a riddle, a riddle ma ree: what is both noun and verb as well as sentence?"

"Noun, verb and sentence?" he repeated to himself under his breath.

Around us it had now become quite dark — the fire lit up his gaunt face, leaving his thin, raddled body in darkness. As he puzzled over the question his face seemed to float —

"Give up?" I asked.

"Yes."

"Silence."

"Silence?"

"Yes, Silence. Silence is a noun, yes?" He nodded. "To silence is a verb, and silence is a sentence."

"How sentence?"

"As in punishment — Livingstone-I-presume — or sanction — you know, *I* silence *you*."

He laughed, "Clever — very clever."

"Another one?"

"Yes."

"What kind of sentence can only be broken, not appealed?" The sound of crickets was now loud around us — I put some more wood on the fire.

"Well, I know now it has to do with silence... and you said that silence was a sentence — one breaks silence, doesn't one?"

"One? *I, me*, Livingstone-I-presume, *I* break *my* silence — the sentence of my silence."

"Oh, yes, I see now."

"But that wasn't bad, Livingstone-I-presume, wasn't bad at all."

We were silent for a while, listening to the sounds of the forest — my silence between us. "Tell me, Livingstone, do you think Silence has an inherent meaning — beyond what words impose... in their absence?"

"I don't believe I understand what you mean."

"Oh dear, oh dear, you are slow — well, we have words, don't we?" He nodded. "But there had to have been Silence before there were words, right?" He nodded again. "Well, that's what I'm interested in — the possible independence of that Silence — independent of word. Is there a philosophy, a history, an epistemology of Silence — or is it merely an absence of word?"

"Oh yes, I see, I see—"

He didn't — I could tell. He was just an old man — tired like me, like me obsessed with discovery — for the sake of discovery, perhaps. We were both silent —

"If I could just draw it, give it a shape, Livingstone-I-presume, make it tangible — would I pattern it like words — could there be a grammar of Silence that I could parse and analyse?

What *is* the logic of Silence?"

"But, my child, you need the word for all that, and there's the rub."

I looked at the tired, pale face, ghostly in the firelight, saw the dying fire, the outline of the tent, the cognac in my shot glass — "I am *not* your child, Livingstone-I-presume," I said very, *very* softly, my tone almost threatening, "and I'm not sure I need words. I'm like you, you see, stubborn. You refused to believe the Zambesi was unnavigable, remember? — from the coast up to the highlands of Shire. I want to make the desert of words bloom — with Silence!"

"Surely you mean the desert of silence bloom with words— "

"You are a hard nut to crack, Livingstone-I-presume, real hard — but crack you will. You remind me of my father — all word, word, and more word — no Silence. It *is* the coarsest of currencies, you know — the word — crass and clumsy as a way of communication; a second cousin, and a poor one at that, of Silence." He looked at me as if I was crazy and went off into one of his sulks again. I let him be while I poured some more cognac and put some wood on the fire. "Now that I have found you — or rather, we have found each other," I said, "I want to ask one thing of you."

"What is that?"

"A kiss— "

He sat up straight — I poked at the fire — "You heard me, Livingstone-I-presume — a kiss — one, small kiss — on the lips — to seal this unholy pact of ours: your Word, my Silence."

All his native, ramrod, Scottish Calvinism, honed in the cold kirks of the highlands, rose like bile in his throat, and he was outraged.

"Relax, Livingstone-I-presume, I have done worse things — a lot worse things — or better, depending on how you look at it — with you... in my dreams." I smiled at him.

He blanched even more, betraying the African sun.

"There is no law against dreaming, is there?" I asked him. "There should be," he muttered, "in cases like this." This coming from the man who had as much as abandoned his wife for his adventures in the "dark continent." Was that a lesser sin than my request for one, small kiss? But his Christian piety was deeply offended.

"Oh, bugger off, Livingstone-I-presume, bugger off." He didn't say anything more for a while. Then he asked, "What is it you want of me?" His words came slowly, almost as if he didn't want to ask them or feared the answer. Or both.

I sighed. I was weary. "Nothing of you, Livingstone-I-presume. But often over the centuries while I searched for you, I would see myself as a shadow, a dark ghost — a memory almost — haunting you in your sleepless nights down throughout the ages — refusing to let you rest in the silence of your lies. Now that I've met you, I don't know — " My voice faded away; then I continued. "What do you know of elephants, Livingstone? You must have seen a few in Africa in your time."

"Nothing," he replied. I could hear the "what now" in his reply.

"Did you know that female elephants send out mating calls to the males at frequencies so low humans can't hear?" I sensed him getting tense again. "Relax, Livingstone — this is not about sex, but just think, your Word, my Silence — matching frequencies so low, so precise only we could hear. Word and Silence — which of the two sent out the mating call, Livingstone, your Word or my Silence? Have you thought of that? Maybe this is about sex after all, Livingstone-I-presume — what do you think?"

He said nothing, his only reply a sound, part sigh and part grunt.

(silence) It grew dark (silence) in the forest (silence) we sat on (silence) he, Livingstone-I-presume (silence) and I (silence) before the dying (silence) embers and my Silence (silence) and all around us was Silence (silence)

One hundred thousand years later, there we were — still sitting before the fire — Livingstone and I and Silence. I stretched out my hand and touched him — he seemed asleep; I shook him gently by the shoulder,

"David, David — are you awake?"

"Hmm, what is it?"

"I want to ask you something— "

"Yes, yes, go ahead."

"When you lay dying... in the swamps of Bangweolo — in your hut — do you remember?"

"Yes, I do."

"What was the last thing you embraced... before you died — your word or your silence... what was it, David, Word or Silence?" And all around us was Silence... and yet more Silence...

How long was it before I prompted him again? "Did you hear me, David?" Perhaps one, maybe two hundred years. "What was the last thing — Word or Silence?"

"Why, I believe it was... "

"Yes, yes," I urged him. "What was it?"

"It was neither word nor silence... but... "

"But what, David?"

"God!... yes, now I see... that is what it was... God! until you asked I never would have... "

"Oh, Livingstone-I-presume, you would have to go and complicate matters further with God, wouldn't you?" And all around was Silence... waiting   patient   content   willing to enfold   embrace   everything   the Word, even.

I couldn't see Livingstone now — so black had it grown

I reached out   my hand   felt the evidence   of SILENCE
all around   around me   original primal   alpha *and* omega
and forever   through its blackness   I touched something
warm familiar   like my own   hand   human   something I
could not   see in the SILENCE   reaching out   through the
SILENCE of space   the SILENCE of time   through the
silence of SILENCE   I touched it   his hand   held it   his
hand   *and* the SILENCE
     I surrendered   to the SILENCE   within

Author's Note

A record of the documents and records of The Traveller, which form the basis of this work, are bound in two volumes, and on deposit at the Bodleian Library, Oxford University. The leather-bound books are burgundy coloured, hand-sewn and of legal size — 8 1/2 by 14 inches. Embossed in gold in the centre of each cover are the words: "Diary of a Traveller." These words are repeated on the flyleaf in a round, strong hand in an ink which is quite faded. Also on each cover, some two inches above the lower edge, and also embossed in gold, are the words "Volume I" and "Volume II"; these words appear on the spines of the books as well. Pasted to the inside cover of Volume I is a hand-drawn map; it reveals the locations of two groups, the ECNELIS and the LENSECI. Various writings and annotations appear on this map, as on all the pages of the diaries. Within the bodies of the books themselves, other maps identify the locations of other groups, some of which are mentioned in this work.

Together the books contain 210 pages of parchment, some of which are crumbling. A large hand covers the pages on one side only, and recounts the journey of The Traveller which is far more extensive than appears in this work.

The diary is arranged in chronological order, according to present calendar time; this conflicts with the time through which The Traveller journeyed. There is an index which lists in alphabetical order, the areas and groups The Traveller visited, and a glossary explaining pronunciation and the meaning of names and words. An appendix (which is typed and appears to have been prepared by someone other than The Traveller), comprises an anthropological description of the groups The Traveller visited, as well as a long dissertation on Silence.

All maps in the books are hand drawn and while some appear crude, many are well-executed, being fanciful and delicately coloured; a few appear to be cautionary tales, told in pictures complete with strange-looking animals and monstrous creatures. Without exception all the maps appear to be well used, some are even worn through from constant handling. The Traveller has covered many, if not all them, with words and notes to herself.

Volume II contains three Polaroid photographs: the first is of an elderly white man standing alone, wearing a pith helmet and white ducks, and carrying a long staff; the greenery around him suggests that it may have been taken in a forest, but the photograph is so faded it is difficult to be certain. Under the photograph appear the words, "Dr. David Livingstone." The second photograph, also very faded, is of two people, one white, the other black, both seated on what appears to be a colourful rug or blanket. A fire burns to their right. They both hold coffee mugs in one hand, and shot glasses in the other. Their features are blurred, but they both smile at the camera. They are identified as Dr. David Livingstone and The Traveller. The third photograph is entirely black, rendering nothing visible.

The chief librarian and archivist at the Bodleian Library believes this to be the original manuscript of the "Diary of a Traveller" and the only extant copy. However, on the last page of Volume II, in the same round hand that appears throughout the volumes, appears the following statement:

This is but a facsimile of my odyssey into Silence. The original diaries, including maps of these travels, were given to the CESLIENS for safe keeping, since they were the only ones who kept their Silence. The exact location of the diaries is unknown, but I believe the CESLIENS have buried them in an unmarked spot.

A brief note on the display case containing these volumes states:

Contrary to the statement on the last page of Volume II, these volumes comprise the only and original copy of the Diary of a Traveller. — William D. Boyd, Chief Archivist and Librarian

A NOTE ON THE TEXT:

Tim Jeal's *Livingstone* (Heinemann, 1973) provided extensive background material on the life and work of David Livingstone. Asterisked quotes in the text are from the *London Journal*, December 1856, quoted in Jeal's work.